The Poet Speaks

Ross Forrest

The Poet Speaks

Ross Forrest

Poems:
The Love Story

My Heart Beats

My heart beats when I see you smile;
My heart beats when I hear your voice;
My heart beats when I hold you;
My heart beats when I hold you;
My heart beats again, because of you.

Essence

The sun rises when she smiles;
Through her heart flows true love;
She is a beautiful mosaic, perfectly placed tiles;
Her aura brings peace as much as a dove;
In her I find true love.

The thought of her brings joy;
Her embrace washes worries away;
In her presence you cannot be coy;
Once in her heart, I plan to stay;
In her I find true love.

Roses get their scent from her;
Time stands still when I am with her;
I will work to be everything to her;
She takes pride in me and I in her;
In her I find true love.

Without You

I would rather be deaf,
And not have heard your voice;
Than to know the beauty of your voice,
And not be able to hear it.

I would rather be blind,
And not have ever seen your face;
Than to know how gorgeous you are,
And not be able to see you smile.

I would rather have no lips,
And never have kissed you;
Than to know how soft and tender they are,
And not be able to kiss you.

I would rather have no sense of smell,
And never have smelled you;
Than to know your scent is of roses,
And not be able to get a whiff.

Lifeless

My heart stopped beating,
My smile began to sag,
My dreams started to fester,
I had lost you.

My future became dim,
My life no longer bright,
My dawn now dusk,
I have lost you.

My incandescence now gone,
My joy now desolate,
My love now pain,
I am empty without you.

Breath

At the sound of your voice,
My heart began to beat.
To hear the symphony composed of your words,
Quiets my troubling pain.

To see your smile,
Is to see Heaven.
To gaze in your eyes,
Is to see an angel.

To hug you and hold you,
Comforts me like a teddy bear.
To feel your warm embrace,
Brings solace and is soothing to my soul.

You compliment all that is great:
You compliment all of me.
I breathe again,
All because of you.

Where Are You

I opened my heart to you,
Now I can't get you off my mind.
For the life of me I don't know what to do;
I ran after you and my love was blind.

Why has my love and heart been designed;
Designed for you and now I am enshrined.
I keep telling people that I resigned;
However, these papers are still unsigned.

I am sitting here with four bottles of brew;
Could careless what people say because my love is
inclined.
Damn shame I feel like I got the flu,
Keep asking God why our love can't be aligned.

Sweetheart, I am on my grind;
Grind, yet my heart stays assigned.
Your boy is truly refined,
To bad this feeling is so unkind.

My army is ready to stage a coup,
Asking why my heart is confined.
Not ready to bid you adieu,
Lady, trust I don't want to be through.

Cast Aside

I woke up reaching out for you;
Your name consumes my every thought.
My color has turned a sad hue,
Why did we have to get caught?

All of me needs you by my side;
This feeling, so true I can't hide.
I pray that one day you will be my bride,
But now I feel my love has been denied;
My heart has become the great divide.

It is supposed to be just us two;
I want to write a different plot.
With you my heart actually grew;
This is not how our love was to be wrought.

I still mention your name with pride.
Your heart is where I should reside;
We were taking this in stride.
Two hearts moving forward allied,
To bad my heart now beats at low tide.

She Speaks of Me

When he speaks to me it is a poem;
Around him, I know my love won't be lonesome.
My heart with him can't be broken;
In his warm embrace, I feel wholesome.

He makes me feel so much love;
I fly in the sky, like a dove.
He fits inside of me like a glove.
I truly declare all of the above.

A beautiful song he sings,
Truly the king of kings.
I adore how his name rings,
Always helping me spread my wings.

This beautiful man is my all,
With him there is no way I can fall.
His head is as smooth as a cue ball;
Hang onto his every word and you will be enthrall.

Questions

Why am I still drawn to you?
Why is my heart with you?
Why do I still think about you?
Why you?

Why can't you let me be?
Why do I still hold the key?
Why am I your detainee?
Why won't you set me free?

Do you still reach out for me?
Do you still want to be with me?
Do you still long for me?
Do you still love me?

Do I want to bid you adieu?
Do you want us to accrue?
Do we have a clue?
Do you think we should start anew?

What You Do

You bring out the best;
You keep me focused on my quest.
You are far better than the rest;
You are touched by God and truly blessed,
For you will design our crest.

With you I must confess.
With you I have to press.
With you I don't have to stress.
With you I can't digress,
For your love won't oppress.

Around you I am complete.
Around you I handle every feat.
Around you I don't have to compete.
Around you I lead the fleet,
For your love is my heart beat.

Beside you I am strong.
Beside you I truly belong.
Beside you I should have been all along.
Beside you I sing a beautiful song,
For beside you I can never be wrong.

Poems:
Inside of Me

I am

I am the Phoenix who will rise no matter how many
times I fall.
I wonder if my work is appreciated.
I hear trees talking to me.
I see an angel protecting me.
I want to love freely and deeply—carelessly;
I am the Phoenix that will rise no matter how many
times I fall.

I pretend to fly like an eagle.
I feel at home in front of the classroom.
I touch the sky when I dream.
I worry about when I will see my youngest daughter,
Isis.
I cry constantly thinking about how long it has been
since I hugged Isis;
I am the Phoenix that will rise no matter how many
times I fall.

I understand love rejoices in truth.
I say right must happen to right.
I dream of a better tomorrow and strive for it.
I try to touch the future.
I hope to bless all around me;
I am the Phoenix that will rise no matter how many
times I fall.

To Ponder

There is so much to say,
I wonder who will listen.
Somethings must stay at bay,
I wonder who will listen.

My mind speaks;
Where will I place the words?
The pen writes;
Where will I place the words?

This heart longs to love—freely;
Who will hold me dearly?
My love rejoices in truth—endlessly;
Who will hold me dearly?

I am more than meets the eye,
So why do I speak with a sigh?
There is more to me than my necktie,
So why do I speak with a sigh?

Am I becoming who I am supposed to be?
Is this the life God designed for me?
Please show me what I need to see?
Is this the life God designed for me?

Scattered

My mind is consumed with thoughts;
My thoughts have consumed my mind.
I am trying to leave them with this pen;
Hoping that I won't sin.

I am blessed to have this energy.
I absolutely love the serenity.
I am grateful for God's gifts, talents, and abilities;
Truly humbled that He continues to protect me.

You dare not judge me!
If only you could see.
Your eyes are wide shut,
So you better hit the cut.

My daughters are my heart,
The reason my day starts,
I love them more than life,
That's why I put up with the strife.

I wonder how long this season will last;
I am ready to make it part of my past.
This rollercoaster needs to end,
That's why I have picked up my pen.

Why, Really Why

Why can't I touch the sky?
Why won't you push until you die?
Why am I at ease when I am high?
Why can't I fly?

Why at times do I feel empty?
Why has aspects of my life made me ennui?
Why can't I always be the emcee?
Why can't I win an emmy?

Why do I think so much?
Why do I hesitate to touch?
Why am I always clutch?
Why won't some of you be a crutch?

Why won't y'all open your eyes?
Why can't I sever ties?
Why don't you hold him when he cries?
Why aren't you there as he tries?

Feel Me

Pen to paper, you can't stop me.
When will you see?
You better back off, I am a bee
Keep trippin, I'll squash you flea.

This is ridiculous,
But I am meticulous.
I can be vicious,
At times I am mischievous.

I can be a thug.
When I drink, I do chug'
But I always need a hug
Trust me, I won't shrug.

I am that guy.
Always reaching for the sky.
Don't know how to be dry.
I got you when I say hi.

Here I am, this is who I is.
I won't stop handling my bizz.
I pass every quiz.
Trust me, I won't fizz.

Preconceive

It is time for you to believe.
Please don't start to grieve.
Trust me, I won't bereave.
All I know how to do is achieve.

There is no time for sick leave.
I won't reprieve.
Not worried how you perceive;
I will always receive.

Roll up the shirt sleeve,
I am ready on any midsummer eve.
Can't get caught in satan's weave,
Because I am always on sabbatical leave.

Pain

I am sitting here with my pen
Lord, please help me not sin
Keep pushing to handle business for my kin
Shit, why am I sitting in this den?

Isis, I am going through a crisis;
It's been over a year since I have seen you Isis.
Your momma uses you as a pawn.
I promise I will be around when it's dawn;
Isis you will always be my fawn.

Where is my baby at?
I am tired of talking about that!
There is no tricks I can pull from my hat.
Promise sometimes I want to pull out my bat.

BITCH, yeah you carned that title!
This is about to move forward without a hitch.
You better call the doctor because this is vital.
There will never be a snitch.
In spite of all you do, you can't stifle;

ME, who always believes,
Could careless what you perceive.
You will drop like dead leaves.
I speak to they who sees.

Rayla Faith

You are my FIRST born daughter,
I need YOU more than I need water.
YOU are truly my Sweetpea;
Your smile has a way to set my heart free.
With you I have nothing to fear.
You are Daddy's dear.
Everything about you is sincere,
Because of you, I see clear!

This Negro

This Negro speaks of things as they are;
Life is more than jewelry, a house and a car.
Step out side the box to see you ain't living up to par;
This Negro speaks because he is a czar.

We spend soo much time at the bar,
How do we do this and think it isn't bizarre?
Sitting over there steadily smoking a cigar;
This Negro speaks because he is a czar.

Always wanting to be the star
All the work we did following the North Star;
To look and see we trying to be a rock star.
This Negro speaks because he is a czar.

Yes, I do watch NASCAR;
Open your eyes, I am the pace car.
You haven't realized you are a freight car.
This Negro Speaks because he is a czar.

In Store

Through the pain and tears, I shall soar;
My life hasn't been easy, but it is no longer a chore.
A broken vessel, but determined to make it to shore;
Day by day at my best times four.

Asking God to break down this door;
Destined to be he who all adore.
When pen hits paper, you can't ignore;
God, your blessings, talents, and grace please pour.

These trials and tribulations have hurt me to the core;
I lay prostrate in prayer across the floor.
All my sins I know I have to pay for;
Thank You Jesus for You will restore.

I have to build a rapport;
Even if I have to stage a world war.
More like it is inside of me and a civil war;
In the end I will smile in galore.

To Be a Twin

To be a twin is to always have a friend.
To be a twin is to share the same skin.
To be a twin is to have love that will never thin.
To be a twin is to constantly grin.

To be a twin is to be the next of kin.
To be a twin means that you shared a bin.
To be a twin is to have a dorsal fin.
To be a twin means you will win.

To be a twin plays better than a violin.
To be a twin you will share a sin.
To be a twin means you can't be a has been.
To be a twin allows you to always have a safety pin.

To be a twin is to have love within.
To be a twin is where life will constantly begin.
To be a twin means your heart is an inn.
To be a twin is to forever have a true friend.

Dear God

I need to know that You hear me.
Please let me know that You are with thee.
Open Your ear to my plea.
I just want to be on a God spree.

You designed this.
I know it won't be all bliss.
Don't let me sink into the abyss.
From You, I just need Your kiss.

You bless me in spite of;
I seek to be Your dove.
You called me to be a labor of love;
I will always praise You from above.

Truly need Your hand,
For I dwell in Your land.
I play only for Your band;
And for You, I will always take a stand.

Take away this sin;
Allow me to grin.
Fill me from within,
For with You I will always win.

Diary of an Addict:

The Poet Speaks

He sighs, feeling frustrated as he gazes out the window and pours another glass of merlot. The wine seems to help him let the words just flow, like a beautiful waterfall in the tropics; however, the words have stopped as if the Earth has stopped revolving. This is not how he functions; this is not how he became great, for this is just not what it is supposed to be. The pressure of fame and dishing out literary masterpieces can take its toll. It was all fun for him when he just wrote for the essence of writing. Now things are different, there are fans, tours, speaking engagements, and critics. He is at his best when he lets the poet speak, no pressure, just pure talent.

"Lord, please," he cries out as the frustration has moved to another level. "What to do," he ponders. The level of frustration continues to rise. "Come on," he states as he gets up from his chair and begins to pace around the cabin. This is the place where he comes to unwind, relax, get into his element, and just marinate; however, at this moment, nothing seems to be working. He bears a similar makeup as the great authors before him: opium, alcohol, sex, these and others have worked for ages. These writers all seem to have their vices; but, for him right now, nothing is working. To remedy the problem, he has locked himself in the cabin, no distractions, no phones, just pen and paper.

"Have mercy!" he exclaims as he sips from his wine glass, still pacing around the cabin. He needs to relax and produce another instant classic. This is what he does; this is who he is, but can he stand the pressure. He always keeps such a calm demeanor, collected, and well put together to those who see him. The only time he lets his guard down is when he is alone, and even then, he is on point and focused on the task at hand. This is his gift, his calling, to touch through the pen. He tells his story, others, and both combined with unmatched style and class. Why can't he get into his rhythm and flow like a lyricist? His poetry has become timeless ballads, his body of work is phenomenal, and he has changed the industry in every way possible; but now, he paces.

"Goodness grief," he utters as he approaches his bar. He grabs a bottle of tequila. What does he expect to get done now? He has been drinking for the past four days; at least he is drinking plenty of water and has been eating the food that he has been cooking in order to perfect the menu that will grace his restaurant. Yes, he is a true artist in every since of the word in every field that he endeavors; but right now, he is lost. He is lost as to where to take this particular character and this particular story.

"What is to come of this person?" he asks as he takes another shot. There is a cigarette hanging from his mouth. His face looks as if he just lost his puppy, and he too is lost. He is a perfectionist, strives for excellence in everything that he does, and is relentless in his pursuit of artistry.

"Well then," he states, for the effects of the alcohol are beginning to hit him. He is binging in hopes of opening that sector of his brain that has allowed him to create such great pieces of literary works, food that keeps customers lined up at his restaurant, and keeps him seeking to rise to another level. "Do most artists go through this?" he questions as he lights yet another cigarette and takes yet another shot. If he would just sit down, go for a walk around the lake, or even go to sleep; not him though, he doesn't stop once he has gotten started there is no end until the end. Is it pure genius or pure insanity?

Nevertheless, he continues to pace around the house, and he takes shots with each pass of the bar. Good for him, he reloaded his bar on his way to the cabin from the city. Nothing is working! The task of writing exceptional pieces of work each time pen hits paper is weighing him down like a military rucksack on a soldier's back after a twenty hour foot patrol.

"When, when will it hit me and flow," he asks searching for the words and story to flow like blood flows through veins; but at this moment, it is like there is a blockage. The blood is struggling to get through and it is jeopardizing his writing life. He is going into shock. CLEAR! He needs a medic to shock him and bring his creative mind back to life.

At this rate, he will have an empty tequila bottle with nothing to show for it. He has already been through three bottles of merlot. "Calm down," he thinks to himself. "It will come to me," he states as the pressure begins to ease. He is breathing easier as if a syringe was plunged into his back to remove fluid from his lungs. "Why am I trppin?" he questions, for he has hit roadblocks before. His pace slows, he takes another shot and is doing breathing exercises as if he is about to give birth.

His eyes now fix themselves on his desk, he grabs a bottle of merlot, and smiles as he approaches his pen and paper like he is gearing up to waltz with his lady. "I'm good!" he exclaims now seated in his chair. Then, pen hits paper.

Empty

He woke up wondering how he got there. Thinking to himself' "Shit, how much did I drink?" as he searches for his cell phones. "How did the night begin? Better yet, how did the night end?" Pondering still on how he got there as he begins to look for his car. This is how his life is shaping up to be. Lost, drunk, high, and confused. At least on this morning, he didn't wake up with some chick.

Gathered together, showered, car located, and in route to get a bottle to take the edge off. His life is being played out one drink and one line at a time. Not particularly how he pictured his life, but he now lives by "it is what it is." It is his norm to have three lines, two shots, and two beers before eleven o'clock in the morning. At this juncture, what does he have to lose that he already hasn't?

Half dazed, still confused, checking receipts to see where he has been as he pulls up to one of his twenty-four hour bars. Pool stick in tow, ready to drink, as he hears his name ringing out as he enters through the doors and approaches the bar. Probably still reeking of alcohol; although, he typically reeks of alcohol and pussy. "You want a shot and beer?" his bartender asks. "Hell yeah!" He dares not be sober, so he does not have to deal with his reality. A reality that illustrates an alcoholic addict who once had it all, but he lost control.

As the shot and beer begin to sink in, his bartender places another round in front of him. "Man, FUCK," he cries out. "Rough night my friend?" If only he knew just parts, he would feel better. "I have no clue, but it is another day." "How did I get to this point," he asks himself. His mornings seem to be lined with questions, and the only answer is cocaine and alcohol.

Another round hits the bar and it ain't even noon. A few more and he'll be on daytime pussy patrol. Searching through text messages, as he takes another shot, trying to get some idea of the day before. He is numb, and it is good for him. Divorce, finding out that he is the father, only working to support his

habits, and on a rollercoaster with his currently

spiraling out of control lifestyle is where he currently

stands. "What to do the rest of the day," he asks as

he racks the pool balls.

Business, Strictly Business

"Snnnniiiiiiiffff, awe that is the shit," he utters as he takes yet another line. He has to get his mind right, for there is business to handle across state lines. He has bathed three times, yet he still has blood on him; it didn't go according to plan. "Stupid bitch wasn't supposed to be there," he states harshly as he continues to clean himself with industrial mechanic soap. "I was to be in and out, hit that muthafucka, and keep it moving," now there are two bodies to clean up, instead of just one.

It had been planned for weeks, "he had to pay for his sins." Hit him when he least expected it, now his eyes are closed. "Snnnniiiiffff, whew SHIT!" he exclaims as he takes a line, a shot of tequila, and gulps his beer. Not looking forward to the trip ahead, but this has been planned too. Leave while the sun is out, handle business at dusk, and be back home by dawn. Looking at him, you wouldn't think that he was capable of such a deed, but he is nothing to play with.

He hops in his car, has to stop by and see the wife, and let her know that he'll be out promoting a new venue. He has such a way with staying calm, cool, and collect. Enters the house, "Honey, I'm home," in that silly kind of way. He kisses his pregnant wife, rubs her belly, and sits down to hear about her day. She is clueless to the fact that he has murdered two people, well handled his business with one, and the other was just a causality of war. They are engulfed in marital bliss; it is a beautiful sight to see.

It is best to dig your ditches a year in advance. The area will be weathered and won't stick out to investigative technology. Commit their location to memory, no GPS, locate, or even Boy Scout etching on trees. Any decent

detective will easily sort those out. Wear your

hunting gear, because you have hunted, animals

that is, all over the region; therefore, an analysis

of dirt, soil, vegetation, insects, and such won't

drive unnecessary attention. Make sure rain is in

the forecast for that evening or next day.

Hurricane and tornado seasons are preferred.

The wait period is essential! The body should

be dry after the three stage bleach soaking and

cleaning. Be sure to rinse thoroughly, the scent

of bleach can be smelled for a great distance.

Wrap the body in plastic and ensure that no parts

touch the transport vehicle. Remember, no duct

tape, it can be traced like a fingerprint.

   After making love to his wife, he showers.

He meticulously shaves the hair from his body;

the process of personal preparation begins. Ever

so mindful to use a body scrub to remove all

dead skin. The process is a necessity; there will

be no traces of him. Dressed appropriately to

leave the wife, it is time to get back to business.

There are bodies to bury and other work to be

done.

The True Affair

"Whew," that felt great is what he thinks

after they both bust another nut. Even if he is

sneaking away from his wife, these moments with her

feel great. They go out to a spot that he is promoting,

have a few drinks, and then tool back to her place to

enjoy passionate sex. There is never a boring

moment with these two. They slide away on lunch

breaks, get together between jobs, and make it do

what they do, great sex and great fun.

This has been going on for some time, at first it

was supposed to be just fun. There was no kissing,

no oral copulation, no holding, but now they are in

deep. They have caught feelings. He has a key to

her place, and now the key to her heart. They are inseparable, with each other like they are married. She even dawns a ring so he can keep his on while they are out and about. She protects him and he her, and the passion is ridiculous.

She comforts him as he deals with his inevitable divorce and drama from his baby momma. He comforts her, makes her feel at ease, holds her till she falls asleep. Even when they get mad at each other, it doesn't last long, they have quietly become one. Where did they turn the corner? How did they get to this point? No more fun and games, it is just the two of them. Lonely when they are apart, wonderful when they are together, heavy between the sheets.

He has met her family; her child responds to him, her father told her to hold on to him, all knowing that he is still married. She has met his family, can call his folks' house, and gets along with those closest to him. Their hearts no longer freezers, but this will not end well. It can't! They are in so deep, point of no return. A bomb will go off in their love affair and they will still be seeking each other, until they point at each other and pull the trigger.

"Baby, you ready to go eat?" he asks as she stares back at him with that look of I want more! There are weekends that they stay in her place and if anyone where to walk in, all they would smell is sex, good sex, no—great sex. Ten, fifteen, twenty times in a weekend, they just don't stop. "Baby, do we have to go eat now?" she asks as she slides her pants down. "I asked if we were going to eat." he mumbles as he fixes his eyes on her crotch. She slowly takes off her pants, slides her panties off, and spreads her legs on the sofa. Her eyes fixate on his, and then on his ever growing arousal. All of her is begging for all of him. She has had to sit on frozen meat after one of their sessions, and will again. "I guess, I am about to eat." he states as he eases towards her. She is dripping in anticipation of what he is about to do.

Ghost

"Really?" he mumbles sarcastically as he gazes out the window. "This is Birmingham, Alabama at its finest." he exclaims. "Am I really seeing this?" he ponders.

"Baby, what are you looking at?" she asks as she is woken by his questions. "Why is it so bright outside?" she utters, wiping the cob webs from her eyes, and easing out of the bed.

"Honey, grab your cell phone!" he exclaims.

"For what?" she questions as she inches towards the window.

"Get your phone sweetheart!" with more vigor in his voice.

"Are you serious?" she erupts as she peers through the window.

"Yes, love this is happening." he states with disbelief in his voice.

"I am getting my phone!" she states now awake, very puzzled, and moving briskly towards the nightstand.

"This will be all over social media, shortly." he states still staring out the window in disbelief.

"Sweetheart, I can't believe this! I promise that I must be dreaming." she ponders.

"I know my dear, as if." sarcastically

spoken.

"Hope the battery is charged enough." she

reports.

"You are only taking a few pictures, my

love." he expresses.

"I am, but I might record this." she states.

For them, it is a once in a lifetime occasion to

witness this. This is not supposed to be

happening anymore, at least not around here.

"Baby, you smell sooo good." sensuously

slips from his lips. He begins to stare through

her nightgown, inhaling all of her scent, as he places his fingertips on her butt.

"Focus Baby!" she replies, but her body moves itself in front of him and is poised for embrace.

"Baby, you know what you do to me." again, sensually from his lips.

"Oh, look the neighbors are on their balcony." she states as she accepts his warm embrace.

"I am still shocked, this is ridiculous." She exclaims.

"I know, I know." he agrees. "This is truly some stuff."

"Who would think to do this?" she questions now snuggled comfortably with him.

"Welcome to Birmingham, Alabama!" he says with enthusiasm.

They are holding each other close, baffled at what they see outside their apartment, well her apartment window. He just pays bills there when necessary. There is something about her scent that causes him to get so aroused. She just adores him and enjoys their time together. It is strange that they are seeing what they are seeing.

"My love," she states.

"Yes, dear," he replies.

"There is a cross burning in the courtyard."

"Yes my dear, in this day and age." he comments. "I'll take care of it." He is going to handle business. No one messes with his peeps or where he lays his head. It is time to handle business.

Hooked

It is a gorgeous day outside, perfect for fishing. There is a lot on his mind, and he needs to relax. He gathers his fishing gear, loads the cooler with beer, places everything in the truck, and heads to the bait shop. Feeling at ease from a night alone in his cabin, he is ready to relax even more. Life has thrown him many wrenches, and he has handled it with true conviction. "Today is going to be a wonderful day!" he exclaims as he eases in the truck.

The staff at the bait shop knows him well; he takes care of them in many ways. Ways that define the other side of him. There are things that he does that no one could ever image by his smooth exterior.

"Good sir, how are you doing today?" the owner states with delight in his voice as he walks through the door.

"Well my friend," he replies.

"It is good to see, it has been awhile." the clerk states. He paces towards the isle with live bait.

"It is always good to be seen, and even better to see y'all." he replies now contemplating over which bait to purchase.

"Let us know if you need any help finding anything." the clerk yells out.

"I shall good buddy." he responds as he grabs what he needs. He approaches the counter, places everything on by the register, shakes hands with the staff members, and hugs the owner.

"Will this be all for you today?" the clerk asks.

"I also need two bags of ice." he states now anticipating his day on the lake.

He pays for his supplies, grabs the bags of ice, and is off to clear his mind. There will be no thoughts of the ladies in his life, the deeds that he has to perform, or anything that has drained him for the past few weeks. A day on the lake, beer to drink, and good fishing ahead is all that consumes his thoughts.

He settles in on the bay and is contemplating if he will fish from shore or grab the boat from the dock. He has a true fisherman's boat, equipped with all the technology to fish the professional's way. He has been fishing since a kid, and he enjoys every part of it. No distractions, nothing on his mind, as he inhales the smell of the lake, and is engulfed by its beauty.

"Ring!" It is his other cell phone, the one that rings when something has to be cleaned up. It is as unexpected as a flat tire on the way to work, but he looks at who is calling.

"Really!" he states. He knows the number well, and he knows that he must answer when called.

"Hello," he answers the phone.

"There is something that needs to be taken care of," the voice on the other end states. "I know that you are out of pocket, but we are on a timeframe to take care of this." The person states with intensity in his voice.

"I understand," he replies.

"Details will follow, stay close to the phone" the person states.

He hangs up and returns to the days planned events. This activity has been planned, for it is one of his escapes.

He works as well as he works because of the way he takes care of his mind. He understands that there must be down time, time for self, and most importantly, space in between each event. There is no reason to draw unnecessary attention. He needs time to himself, so that he can focus on what he

inevitably has to do.

The day will go as planned, but he understands

that duty calls.

Is This Real?

He has just enjoyed a great time with her, she might not be one hundred percent his, but her heart belongs to him; on the other hand, he is truly single, wants to be only hers, for he is soo enchanted by her. They have only been at this for a few months, but it has intensified deeply. Before it got started, they discussed the rules of engagement, for he knew she was married. How did it get started, well as soon as he walked into the room, she had all of his attention, and he was fixated on her beauty, her smile, and that infectious personality can explain it all. Neither knew at that time where the relationship was going to go,

He got a text message from her, he responded. (Yes, numbers were exchanged, for he is smooth with what he does.) He felt that this was the chance to show his true interest in her. He text back, flirting ever so slightly. She reads the text and wonders if he is flirting, but she is a bit naive. Cute in her naivety and that attracts him even more. She responds innocently, questioning where he is going with this. It is time for him to lay down the charm and smile through every text.

She is standing there wondering if he is flirting. Luckily her niece is with her, and she explains the deal. Now the tension turns up, hearts beating on both ends. They have both been waiting for this moment for weeks, and it is finally here. They both pause, and question what to say and what to do. He is a man, chivalrous, but still a man. He tests the water.

Texting, "So when can we hook up?"

She text back, "What do you mean?"

"I find you attractive & would love 2 kiss those lips." he replies.

She is smiling and intrigued as she reads his text, wondering why a man like him would ever mind her the attention that he is giving her. She focuses; she doesn't want to get started on wrong foot.

"I need to tell you something." she text.

"Listening," he responds. He is hoping that he hasn't pushed too hard, but trying to remain cool. He awaits her response.

"I'm just a live in," she text back.

"Huh," he states, now he is total confused.

"I told you that I was married, but I am just his live in." she responds back.

"Live in? So you two aren't married?" he text back with true excitement.

"Nope!" She too doesn't want this opportunity to pass bye. He has such an air about himself, captivates all that are around him, and he speaks like poet—music to her ears. She doesn't want to come off as easy, a slut, or a cheater; for she hasn't cheated on the guy she lives with.

"EXCELLENT!!!!" he replies now his heart is beating. "What to say next?" he questions as he smiles from ear to ear. She is a gorgeous lady, breathtaking in every way.

Her niece echoes in her ear, "As fine as he is, you best not let him slip!"

"I know, I know," she exclaims as she draws pictures in her head.

He is more excited than her, truly beautiful, truly intelligent, truly a catch for any man, but he feels he is the right man. He anticipates what is going to happen next. He is methodical, calculated, obsessive compulsive, and hyperactive, things have to be done accordingly; however, when it comes to her, he is completely vulnerable, for she is truly the essence of beauty.

The text messaging continues for hours. They are giggling and smiling from ear to ear with anticipation of what could happen next. It is a feeling that neither have felt in many years to truly be excited and enjoying good conversation.

As excited as she is, she ponders on why he would be interested in her. She questions, "I wonder if this is his sibling or friend playing a trick on me." She is getting anxious, but won't let it hamper where this is leading. "I so want to kiss him," she thinks to herself. Little does she know, he is thinking the same thing, he wants to kiss her too.

He will not let the opportunity to kiss her pass him the next time that they see each other. "How can I ask her for a kiss," he asks himself. He gets nervous when it comes to someone that he is truly interested in. "I just have to ask her," he states as he grabs his cell. "Lets see, what to say," he thinks as he stares at his cell.

"Beautiful Lady, I want a kiss," he text.

"Certainly!" She replies with her eyes very wide and full of excitement.

"I won't tell you when, but I will kiss you when I see you," he texted in response to her text. He is feeling the butterflies in his stomach.

"This better be him!" she exclaims as she too begins to feel the butterflies.

They will have to wait until the next evening when their schedules align. The feeling they have is truly of glee, and they can't wait to see each other. Time won't move fast enough, for they have been waiting for this moment for weeks.

It happens, they kiss and it is better than both could have ever imagined. Their heartbeats accelerate, breathing intensifies, and body temperatures rise as they kiss ever so passionately.

This is truly going to be the road never taken.

Klassic Car

She woke up mad as hell. "Who does he think he is," she exclaims! "How in the world does he think I will ever be the second lady, mistress, or just sex," she utters with authority. "I am worth more than this!" she demands. "I am going to handle business," she demands. He is wonderful man, but her heart is worth more than the stupidity that he brings to the table.

He has no idea what he is about to walk into. He enters her place as if all is well. Beyond his thoughts, she has been thinking to long and that is dangerous. She is dangerously in love, opened her heart to him, and he played her for a fool.

"Hello Baby," he greets her as he enters the house.

"Hey Sweetheart," she replies as if all is well. In her mind, she is contemplating how she will let him know that she is number one, second to none.

"How was your day, my dear?" he asks as if everything is kosher.

"My day was wonderful," she responds, yet gathering how she is going to leave her mark on him. He will know that he has messed with the wrong lady.

"You want to go for a ride, my dear?" he asks, hoping she wants to ride in the freshly restored 64'

GTO. It is his prize possession, other than her—his trophy lady.

"Sure, Baby that would be nice." She states as she searches for clothes to wear for a night out on the town. She does enjoy every moment with him.

"Lets run through town, grab a bite, and have a few drinks; he is anticipating a great evening with her. She is putting on the correct outfit as he takes the opportunity to put some snow up his nose.

"Snnnniiiiffff," is the sound of him snorting cocaine to be on the level he feels he needs to be on to truly enjoy the evening. He takes another line, has a shot of tequila, and sips on a beer as she gets herself ready for the evening. He does his best to hide his habits from her, and she is blinded by his love.

They ride around town, fresh as fresh, sexy as sexy, and on point in many ways. The car is pearl white, sleek, looks stock; but the wheels, the stance of the car, and sound she makes as the throttle is pressed lets all know that she owns all eyes and all asphalt. He has spent four years getting her together, and now she is on the road. They are enjoying the ride and each other. Love is a wonderful thing.

It is time to impress the town and let them see a true driver's car, so they pull up to one of his spots. He drops her off at the front door like a true gentleman and with true chivalry. He remarks,

"Baby, I am gonna go park, wait for me here."

"Okay love," she slightly forgets about her true

intentions.

It is his chance to let his nose sky another line or

three, and be right for the night. He has to be able to

stay up for the duration of the night. His mind is all

on her, and he believes that her mind is all on him.

They have been together for a minute—a long time.

He has allowed her to hold his heart, and she has

allowed him to hold her heart.

He has strategically parked the 64' and is

approaching the bar. As he gets close, she is standing

waiting on his arrival, fully engulfed by his being as he approaches her.

"You ready Love?' he asks as he clasps her hand and they walk up the four steps to the entrance. They are at a spot that he has been patronizing for fourteen years. It is his "Cheers." It is the bar that he feels at home when he is there, and he never takes just anyone to this spot. Therefore, she is with him because she is special, she is his heart.

"Yes dear, I am ready," she remarks with a smile on her face feeling his aura and the love that seeps through his hand that is grasping hers. She does truly love him, and he does truly love her.

They are doing it his way: shots of tequila, drinking America's finest beer, laughing, and listening to great music all with genuine smiles on their faces. The evening couldn't be more perfect.

He feeds the jukebox with money to keep the mood right. He knows that the evening is going to end with fireworks from their bed. He truly loves her; she is the apple of his eye, the one that has been his true support.

The evening could not have been better: drinks, music, dancing, and all smiles. It is time for them to get back to the house; interestingly, the tab is paid without him paying a dollar, for he knows the owner well. They ride back to the house in true bliss; he has no clue that she knows what he did just a few night

ago.

They arrive at the house; there is nothing to drink when he wakes up and all the substances he has consumed wear off. She is about to fix some sweet tea. Damn, she remembers her true intentions. She acts as if she is making sweet tea, but the sugar, the sugar ends up in the gas tank of the 64'!

Say Amen

The choir takes their seats as the reverend

approaches the pulpit. It is time to preach, this is

God's time. He removes all of him, so God can take

over. He bows his head to pay homage to God's

house. He sighs, takes a deep breath, it is time for

God to show up and show out.

"Let the church say AMEN." He gathers

himself. He has a cold sweat and is shaking, but gives

himself to God so His work can be done.

"Let us pray," he mumbles, nerves shot and

worried how the next fifteen minutes are going to go.

"My Father and my God, for the blessings you

continue to bestow, I say thank You." still shaking

and nervous as he prays. "For just this moment, Lord have Your way. Remove all of me and speak to Your people. We need a word from You. Father God, forgive me of my sins, so that I may deliver Your message. I am just a broken vessel trying to make it to shore. Nevertheless, when it is all said and done, You shall receive all the glory, honor, and praise regardless of how this message goes. I am Your tool, use me Father God. Amen!"

He adjusts himself, ready for God to speak through him. He speaks, "If you have your life manual with you, turn to the Gospel according to Mark, chapter fourteen, and starting with verse twenty-three." He takes a breath and then lets God speak. "It reads: Then he took the cup, and when He had given thanks He gave it to them, and they all drank from it. And He said to them. 'This is My blood of the new covenant, which is shed for many. Assuredly, I say to you, I will no longer drink of the fruit of the vine until that day when I drink it new in the kingdom of God." He is about to preach; now feeling in his element. "Lord!" he states as the sermon is about to flow.

"PREACH REVEREND!" echoes out as he gets himself together. He ran from God for seven years, thought he was in the clear; but no sir, God had plans for him before he was born. He is a leader of man, a preacher for preachers, a teacher for teachers, he is

God's chosen! The sermon is under way. "God has

a way of always preparing us for what is to come." he

states with true conviction. "All that we may

encounter in life, God will sit us down at the table

and break bread with us, as He prepares us for what

is to come." He is feeling more comfortable, the

Spirit of the Lord is upon him. He continues to

preach.

Sermon goes as planned, time to bring it to a

close. He preaches, "I wait for the day that God parts

the sky, and Jesus places one foot on nowhere, and

the other foot on nothing, as He calls all His people

home. Yes, that is the day that I want God to say 'job

well done, you ran your race, and I am proud of you!'

YES LORD, today You make me whole. For you carried the cross, they crowned You with thorns, they stretched You wide on the rugged cross, even pierced your side; but on that DAY, YOU got up with all power in Your hands! Yes Lord, the sun didn't shine until the SON shined! You Father God, and only You, make a way out of no way." He returns to his seat, completely engulfed by the presence of God.

The doors of the church are open, five people join that day. He gives all the glory to God, and then he returns to being him.

Reality (Breakthrough)

"It wasn't supposed to be like this," he ponders as he wakes up under a bridge. Unable to get into his place of residence, no car, no one left to turn to. He has run everybody off: family, friends, church members because he refused to change, get right, and fly straight. "This has got to change," he demands! A stint in rehab, jobless, lost dignity, a lost sense of self, and now he is here. He is highly educated and highly ignorant. He is smarter than smart, and dumber than dumb. At one point he was on top of the world with a gorgeous wife, beautiful children, highly respected, and now nothing.

When reality hits, it hits harder than a freight train moving at full speed through a concrete wall. He is now that wall that was just hit by a train. "Thank you Lord for my health, strength, my mind, and a corner to pray in," he prays as he pulls himself together. No money for alcohol, tired of the cocaine, and truly sober. It is time to start somewhere, anywhere but here. It was time for him to start somewhere, he had to get back to his roots, and move from there. Through him, many lives are going to be touched in positive ways. He has a calling on his life, and thank God that the perseverance stays kicking in.

"Time to get back to me, no, time for a better me." He began to put together a success routine, a fail proof way to better himself every day. The road was not going to be easy. Friends were going to be lost; but in the end, he would stand tall and shine bright. He was designed to dominate, strive for perfection in all that he does. Day by day, hour by hour, minute by minute, second by second he is determined to rise from the ashes and soar to new heights.

Stopping himself from crying out "why oh why did I take this path" as he designs a new look. Life is what we make it, but he made his life extra rough, climbing the rough side of the mountain. He went down a slippery slope, but is determined to stand on top of the world. The women, parties, and rock star life is no longer appealing. "Shit, this will make me a valuable asset to many," he claims as he asks God for his gifts and talents to be restored. He is the true definition of a phoenix; no longer will he be defined by who he used to be.

A seed has been planted, only those with his best interest at heart will be able to water the soil. There is no time to focus on what could have been, what was, where he could be. The process of forming the diamond is about to end. The process of cutting rough edges, polishing the entire surface has begun, and now he will be perched on platinum. He now speaks, "there is nothing that you can't accomplish, buckle your boot straps, and handle business." The journey isn't going to be easy, but this bird will sing a beautiful song—soon.